Thunderers' Hunt

Cathy Smith

ISBN: 9798230499824

Contents

Thunderers' Hunt

It was almost time for the yearly Wild Hunt, and the Allfather had a special quarry in mind. Odin took Thor up to his high seat, Hjaldskaf to show him a man trekking across the ocean instead of sailing it. He also invited Loki to observe the sight.

"His slippers can't be too impressive, even if he can walk

on air. I'd be running with my skywalking boots not trudging." Loki laughed. He demonstrated his words by lifting off the floor.

"See what you can do to scout the man out. I want to see what his intentions are," Odin said.

Loki glanced down at the dot on the ocean. "It's one man treading water, not a war fleet."

"Perhaps, he's the sole survivor of a war fleet? That would make him a suitable quarry for the Wild Hunt. Jormungander defends his territory and acts as a guardian in the Northern Sea." Odin said.

Loki's brows drew together. "Guardian? You made him the Guardian of the Northern Sea?"

Odin sighed, “He doesn’t allow intruders in his territory. He’s the guardian by default.”

“I can always ask Jormungander who this man is?”

The Aesir had thrown his son in the sea when he grew into a monstrous serpent. He was the best choice of an ambassador for them.

Odin sighed. “See what you can find out.”

***

Loki’s seagull skin was less glamorous than the Asynjur’s bird skins. Yet, this skin was appropriate for his assignment. He could transform into a salmon, but that was only good for fresh water. Not to mention there was the risk Jormungander would mistake him for a meal. He spent a day flying and called on Ran and Aegir for a night's lodging when his arms became sore.

Ran was trawling for mollusks with her net when he saw her. She opened up their shells to pluck pearls out of them before throwing them back into the sea. She was building up a pile of pearls with this method.

He landed next to her, and she shooed him away with her knife. "Ran," he began.

She threw an opened mollusk shell in his direction with its flesh bared. “Here’s a meal for you, Loki.”

Loki shifted to his regular form. “Raw oysters don’t count as proper hospitality for an ambassador of the Aesir.”

Her brows rose. “I thought you were avoiding them again. Sparing a mollusk for a seagull is less dangerous than giving succor to one who is out of favor with the Allfather.”

“The Allfather’s pledged to always find a seat for me at his table.” Loki shrugged and grinned as he said this.

“Does he want Aegir to send a cask of beer?” Ran asked.

"No, I just want to ask you about the location of the Midgard Serpent. He hasn't been guarding the western borders of late."

Ran's seashell cups jiggled with laughter. "Does the Allfather want to charge Jormungander with deserting his post? He only guards that border because he's defending his territory. He couldn't care less about Midgard."

"Did he get bored? Has he gone into hibernation?" Sometimes Jormungander's coils floated up and layers of dirt and plants grew on them as he slept.

"He was chasing some explorers the last time I saw him.

They came back. He didn't." Ran said.

Loki frowned. "Did they slay him?"

"They went over the horizon. I assumed they dropped off the world, but the explorers came back. They were lesser in number and complaining of hostile natives in a land they called Vinland. I was so curious for the news I let them pass me by while their skald composed the Vinland Saga.

My daughters wanted me to collect the sailors in my net. However, I wanted to hear the story so much I let them pass while the skald sang each new stanza he made each night. Before I knew it they passed out of my territory."

"What did the skald say of Jormungander?" Loki asked her.

"He shadowed them when they were in the deep sea. They didn't mean to travel so far into the depths. The explorers thought they were safe because they kept in sight of land. The ship's passengers were traders and farmers looking for land to settle on. Erik the Red told them of a land to settle beyond Iceland, and they wanted to find it."

"That's why they sought to travel in sight of coasts. There was one island in the distance, full of green grass. The grass grew lush, but the island was too small for more than one person to settle on. Yet, it gave them hope they were coming to a coast with good farmland. However, they kept seeing an island chain of grassy knolls"

The passengers feed for their cattle ran low. Eventually, the day came when meant to go ashore on the grassy islands to give the beasts pasture.

However, rocks appeared on the grassy isles. They were so sharp that the crew feared bringing their longship ashore. 'Where's the farmland Erik the Red promised us?' Olaf the merchant asked.

Soon the passenger's provisions were becoming sparse. Yet Olaf the merchant still remained fat. He refused to share his vittles with the other passengers. He had the best quarters on the ship and kept his door closed to them to hide himself from their pinched faces."

Ran exchanged a knowing smile with Loki, who rubbed his hands together. Such conditions as she described were the prelude to a bloodbath. No Viking would starve if a civilian refused to share their food with him.

"The passengers were making plans for Olaf when they saw an island with the biggest rocks yet.

It had two rounded boulders, and the Captain said. 'Hold off your plans for Olaf, we need him to pay our toll to cross these waters.'"

The round boulders moved to reveal two great serpent's eyes. The captain stood at the prow of the ship and hailed the Midgard Serpent. They spoke in a language that none of the passengers understood though I think it was suspicious myself. However, the passengers accepted this. They assumed the Captain picked up the tongue in one of his voyages.

Olaf emerged from his rooms when he saw they stopped moving.

"What's the meaning of this? Why aren't we moving forward?"

The Captain turned to face him with a smile. "We have to pay the Midgard Serpent a toll for crossing his waters. I've promised him a landwhale."

"We have no such thing in our manifest." Olaf said.

"No, but there's a landwhale listed on our passenger list." The Midgard Serpent lunged forward. He swallowed Olaf the Merchant whole while the Captain laughed.

The passengers cowered in fear. Jormungander spit up Olaf's gold armbands on the deck and re-submerged. He drenched everyone on deck with this movement. The island chain they followed disappeared from sight. That's when they realized they'd been following his coils.

"We've paid nine days' worth of toll. Jormungander will want another landwhale when the nine days are up," the captain said.

The crew strove to find land during those nine days. On the tenth day they raced to avoid the Midgard Serpent. Just when it looked like they could outpace him, there was a squall. The water churned around them. They saw the serpent and a fellow passenger flung about in the water.

The sea serpent accepted the overboard passenger as a toll.

He gave them another nine days' passage in the waters. The waters stilled. That's when they knew Jormungander was using his tail to agitate the water."

Loki laughed, "It sounds like Jormungander was having his own wild hunt."

She paused to pry a pearl out of a mollusk shell and snorted. "Then the fool captain cuffed the bard and told him to shut up before he could finish the story."

The bard said, 'But people need to know of Jormungander's Saga in Vinland.'

'Then let the Midgard Serpent sponsor you. You need to sing for your supper, not spread tales of cowardice and infamy,' the Captain said.

"So the skald sang some insipid song that put me to sleep, and the longship away drifted from view." Ran sighed at this.

Loki chuckled, "It's too bad the skald wasn't Bragi Biarkison. He would've composed the ballad, anyway."

"Bragi Biarkison?" Ran frowned.

"He's from the human's upstart Bjorn's line. Bjorn chased Rig off when he tried to father one of the three classes of men on his wife. Bragi Biarkison wanted to be a skald but refused Odin's price for a double portion of mead." Loki said.

"What was the price?" Ran asked.

"Betray his sire Berserk's Bane Biarki in battle." Loki said.

Ran's brows rose, "And he refused to betray his sire for such a bribe. That sounds like a lineage to be proud of."

"Many jotun runts think so to. They've intermarried with Bjorn's descendants."

"Intermarried?" Ran asked.

"Jotun grooms pay proper brideprices for the human women of this line. Jotun fathers entrust their marriageable midget daughters to these men." Loki said.

Ran shrugged. “It sounds like the best matches the runts and midgets can hope to make for themselves. It’s different for my daughters. They can do better.”

“Aye,” Loki said.

“Though this skald who makes compositions others dare not sounds useful. I’d let him sing for his supper in my hall.”

Loki smirked, “As opposed to making him your supper?”

She cackled at this. She could change her shape into a shark when she wanted. Though most folk in the Nine Worlds preferred her mermaid form. Ran smirked toothily at the memory of the appetites she indulged in with her shark form.

“Thanks for your help. I know more than I did before. Perhaps, this little man walking across the sea can tell me where Jormunganđer went.”

Ran nodded. “Stop by and tell me the tale if you find out the Midgard Serpent’s wyrd.”

Loki shivered. The word “wyrd” made it sound like Jormungander’s life had ended, and his story was set.

***

The view from Hjaldskaf made everyone in the Nine Worlds a speck. It was hard to tell how tall the wanderer was, but Loki suspected the man was short. "Jormungander is capable of taking care of himself against a dwarf." Loki assured himself as he flew to meet the trekker.

He had to assure himself. Loki wasn't be involved in the day-to-day life of his bairns. However, that didn't mean he wouldn't care if one of them got injured or died.

Jormungander was the stoutest of his sons, and he was the last one Loki thought he'd have to worry about. Had the boy gotten bored with biting his tail and swam to new waters? Loki was never content to stay in any place too long, and he could understand this. "It's not as if we're so close he'd tell me if he was leaving for new waters."

He usually told Sigyn and their boys when he was leaving Asgard. He never told them where, though. Half the time he had a direction and not a destination in mind. Other times Odin gave him an assignment he ordered Loki to be discreet about. Sigyn often told herself he was busy on some commission from the Allfather if she hadn't heard or seen him in a while.

Eventually he found the trekker and circled around him. The man was short but stocky, with muscles all over. His legs were more toned than his arms, which showed he didn't work at a forge. Loki let out a caw at the sight of the man's clothing. He wore leather. The shoes were thick slippers of deerskin.

Loki would've preferred a proper boot himself, but the leather slippers weren't useless. The man wasn't walking on the waves so much as stepping half a foot above them.

They must be like my skywalking boots. He could walk on air with them too. He shed his seagull skin to show off the superiority of his boots.

The man paused in his trek. More out of politeness rather than marveling at this show of shapeshifting and magic. He didn't cry out in alarm, and he allowed Loki to approach him.

Loki was able to make him out better as he came closer to the man. He snorted when he saw the man carried flint-tipped arrows that even a mortal's mail shirt could deflect.

The man allowed for this inspection. He met him in the eye, but without glaring at him. He acted as if surveying the threat potential of a stranger was a natural thing. Loki stared at him for a long time with no response since the man refused to be insulted or threatened by him.

The Trickster's heart sped up when he saw the man wore a snake skin vest. It was made from a snake skin as thick as the mailshirts dwarven smiths made. Those scales would've been living armor on the serpent they were taken from.

Is it Jormungander's hide? He wondered to himself.

Of course, Jormungander shed his skin regularly, so the vest need not be a hunting trophy. Especially not with those flint-tipped arrows.

"Wassail," he said.

"Sago," the man said back.

Loki's brows came together, "What does 'Sago' mean?"

The man took a pouch from his belt. It contained an herb and a small clay horn that was hollowed out. He watched as the man took a pinch of the herb with one hand and placed it in the hollow horn with the other. The man snapped his now free hand and sparks flew from it to alight the herb.

Its pungent scent made Loki sneeze. The man placed the clay horn to his lips and inhaled. Then he blew a ring of white smoke in his face. Loki's face turned red as he gave a series of hacking coughs.

He stepped away from the man, and said, "Fine, be that way."

Before he flipped his seagull skin coat over his head and blew off.

***

Ran was counting her pearls by the time Loki came back to speak to her. “You’re back.” she said, glancing at Loki as he took off his cloak. “Did you hear what happened to Jormungander?”

“I’ll have to put off my personal business for later. I come on business for the Allfather. He’s inviting you to take part in this year’s Wild Hunt.”

Ran shook her head, “We’re not leaving the sea to journey into some forest.”

"The prey is on the sea. You and your daughters will get first crack at him." Loki said.

"On the sea?" Ran asked.

"The coward thinks we won't be able to reach him if he's not inland." Loki rubbed his hands together.

Ran shook her head. "Drofn likes sinking ships. I'll let her play with the Wild Hunt's prey."

Loki chuckled at this.

***

Drofn used the form of a dolphin to greet the visitor. She chose to stick her head above the water and chatter at the wee man.

He stopped in his tread to look at her. Once Drofn got his attention, she dipped her head to swallow some water than to spurt it out of her blowhole.

He stepped aside to avoid the spurt, and Drofn screeched when she saw he was going to ignore her. She kept the dolphin tail but shifted her top half to look like a maiden.

Drofn tugged at his breeches in prelude to dragging him down. She couldn't care less if he was fool enough to think it was in prelude to bedsport. He stomped on her hand and the air crackled with a thunderboom. A spark went off between with a loud zap. Drofn yelped in pain and retreated.

Loki watched this from a bird's-eye view in his seagull skin. The exchange was a subtle brush-off. Perhaps the little man let Drofn off easily because she was a maiden? What would be capable of against a fellow warrior?

***

Drofn wasn't ready to give up. She came back riding her favorite kraken beast. Its tendril wrapped around the man's leg.

He rose higher, out of the kraken's reach.

The kraken rose from the water to follow him, proving to be an island sized squid. Loki cackled when he saw the wee man aim a flint-tipped arrow at the sea monster. This gesture of defiance was futile.

Drofn shook with sadistic laughter herself at this sight. Her laughter turned to shrieks when the arrow launched.

The arrow ripped through the air with a crackle. It flashed with a fierce white light and boomed when it struck the kraken senseless. Drofn shrieked and fled underwater.

The kraken's flesh crackled and fried in the water, so it

was nothing more than seafood. Indeed, the man regarded it as such when he hacked at the kraken's limbs off and chewed on it. He must've liked it, for he chopped off more limbs and cut them into strips of jerky.

Loki watched with horror-stricken eyes. He wondered if this happened to Jormungander in Vinland?"

***

Odin must've been watching from Hjaldskaf. He was aware of what happened in the sea and called a Thing at Gladsheim.

"The man will make landfall within nine days at his current rate of progress." Odin told the Aesir at the Thing.

"We can always make him the prey for our latest Wild Hunt when he hits the land." Loki said.

"Do you want him to reach landfall at all? I can shoot him before he reaches land." Uller said. He was the Aesir's best hunter and preferred to hunt in winter, though he made an exception for the Wild Hunt.

"Not if I get him first," Skadi said. The jotun maiden was also a keen hunter with bow and arrow.

Loki smirked. "Why should you two have all the fun?"

Frigga shook her head. "Don't underestimate this man."

"Do you think he's a jotun? We can always call Thor back from Jotunheim."

Frigga nodded "yes" at this. "Do it. It's the only way to assure a peaceful resolution to this."

***

Uller and Skadi used the man as target practice when he was visible from the shore. They positioned themselves on branches of a sapling of Yggdrasil. Skadi shot first and aimed for his heart, but the man's snake skin vest deflected her arrow.

Loki hovered above this scene as a seagull. He groaned at the sight of the deflected bows.

Only Jormungander's hide was so tough.

The man moved so fast that Uller's shot at the head missed him. He was as fast as a flicker of lightning. Though he trekked at a moderate pace for his journey across the water. When he reached shore, he landed on the earth. Then he stomped his foot underneath the tree. A current of lightning traveled up the trunk and split it. Uller and Skadi spilled out senseless onto the ground.

The two didn't have time to respond and fell down with loud thuds. Skadi was too stunned to move when she landed close to him. The man wasn't stomping, but she twitched from the currents expelled by his feet. The little man looked down at her and humphed.

He lifted his feet above the earth to stop the currents of electricity that flowed from his body. Then he moved on towards Asgard.

***

Thor came back to Asgard the next day. He laughed at the sight of the little man marching towards Yggdrasil when Odin pointed him out. "Can you deal with this midget?"

Thor laughed so hard at the sight of the man it set off a thunder boom in the sky. "People will be saying I've become a coward if I switch from fighting jotuns to midgets."

"He held his own against one of Ran's daughters when she tried to drag him down. He fended off Uller and Skadi when they tried to use him for target practice." Odin said. "He may be a jotun in disguise."

Thor's brows furrowed. "Jotuns can't stand to shape change into anything smaller than a tall human. That man is almost as small as a dwarf."

"We've known dwarves to be troublesome. Alvis tried to carry off your daughter, Thrud, didn't he?"

Thor sighed.

***

The little man trudged closer, and Odin saw he was coming to Bifrost. Loki followed the little man in seagull form.

Odin knew it wasn't good to be the focus of Loki's attention. Yet, he seemed only to follow him.

He went to Asgard's Gate to speak to Heimdall. Heimdall's senses were so keen he didn't need a high seat like Hjaldskaf. He could already see what was happening in the Nine Worlds without it.

"Loki goes wild doing the Wild Hunt. Do you know why he's holding back?" Odin asked Heimdall.

"He's not holding back. He keeps casting runes and there's the smell of smoke every time he tries and fails." Heimdall said.

"Smoke?" Odin frowned.

"The man carries an herb in a pouch. It has a fragrance when it's fresh and a different scent when he burns it. I don't know what they call this herb. Though its scent is distinctive, even if it's unlike anything I've smelled before."

"Strange," Odin said. "This Wild Hunt is unlike any we've had before.

***

Odin's curiosity about the herb made him wait for an opportunity to test the power of the herb. He waited on Hjaldskaf for the right opportunity. It came when the man took out his pouch of kraken tentacle jerky and a bottle of rain water at midday.

He took out a flint knife and Odin murmured a rune to dull its edge since he figured it still counted as a blade. A fragrance filled his nostrils and made him cough for several moments. The man finished his lunch by the time Odin found his breath again.

***

When the man reached Asgard's Rainbow Bridge, Bifrost he set up a camp and lit a fire at its base. He seemed content to wait.

"We'll be obligated to provide him hospitality if he comes to Asgard's gates. I want to make sure it doesn't happen." Odin said to Thor.

Thor shrugged and said, "So be it."

He walked down Bifrost fully armed but not brandishing Mjolnir. This was as close to friendly as Thor got with strangers. He acted as an escort for the Allfather.

The man threw some of his herb on the fire at the sight of their party.

Its scent was so strong Thor rocked as the fumes hit him. The man spoke some words, and Odin wondered if they were a charm.

“What’s wrong?” Odin asked as Thor blinked his eyes.

“He gave me a blot,” Thor said.

Odin looked at the fire. The herb was now white ash. “I don’t see any animals or blood.”

“I know, but the herb’s strong enough to do the work of a blot.” Thor strode up to the fire. He carried his hammer on his belt but didn't brandish it. When he was in hearing distance, the two talked to each other.

The two acted like they understood each other. Even if Odin could only understand Thor's side of the conversation.

Thor's part of the conversation disturbed Odin

"I am Thor the Thunderer of the Aesir...You are Boomer of the Haudenosaunee Thunder Beings and their Runner." He said aloud.

The man presented Thor with a strand of white beads and a pouch full of the herb. He opened the pouch to throw more of the herb on the fire to show its purpose. Thor inhaled the fumes with a deep sigh.

"There is a Great Horned Serpent who came across the water to Turtle Island....He was adopted into a clan of monster serpents and named their war chief... He has a wife, and they are breeding an army of warriors ...They hibernate each winter and emerge hungry in spring."

"You are inviting me to your next hunt in the Spring."

Thor turned to Odin. "I'm inviting him to Bilskirnir tonight and will escort him into Asgard."

Odin frowned. The Aesir were oathbound not to shed blood in Asgard. The Wild Hunt was over.

***

Thor gave Boomer a meal at Bilskirnir before he left to go back home. He understood the man though they had to burn the herb in a soapstone dish Boomer had in his pack.

The man's courtesy was alien to Thor but not so incompatible they might as well be enemies. His daughter Thrud acted as hostess for the dinner. She, too, was drawn to the tobacco. Boomer accepted her presence at the table without comment.

Boomer said. "The Onkwehon:we use tobacco to speak to us and their Creator. I thought I might be able to speak to your people's thunderer if I carried some with me."

Thor opened the medicine bundle Boomer gave him and saw it had seeds. "That's to give to your faithkeepers to grow tobacco for their gardens."

"Why would I give such a potent plant to them?" Thor asked.

"Indian Tobacco is most potent to us when it's given as a burnt offering by human beings. They throw the leaves in their fires whenever they hear thunder." Boomer said.

"I'll see if I can get my followers to use it for blots. Some of them are farmers," Thor said.

Thrud took the packet. "Let me grow the first harvest before we give seeds to your followers on Midgard, Father."

Thor's brows rose. Thrud was a Valkyrie and preferred to collect slain warriors for Valhalla. Her mother had never gotten her to grow flowers in the gardens. It was strange that she deemed this tobacco plant worth the effort.

They served Boomer his goats as the main dish. Boomer accepted what they offered and Thrud gave him a drinking horn of mead.

“They taste like venison.” Boomer said with a twitch of his nose as he laid a bone onto the skins of his goats.

“You don’t like venison?” Thor felt for his hammer.

“Our women eat venison. We Haudenosaunee Thunder Beings prefer the flesh of the serpents we hunt. Though we hunt venison for our Onkwehon:we wives.” Boomer said.

This time Thor wrinkled his nose. “Is eating the serpent’s flesh a sign of bravery among your people.”

Boomer shrugged. “The Haudenosaunee have a tradition of eating the flesh of their enemies during times of war. Though the Creator wants to stop the custom among the Onkwehon:we.

Thor frowned. “Who are the Onkwehon:we?”

“The human beings on Turtle Island.” Boomer said.

Thor shook his head. Thinking it was just as well Loki couldn’t understand Boomer’s speech. He’d want to avenge his son if he believed Jormungander was killed and butchered in Vinland. *They truly must be savage if even their mortals eat their enemies’ flesh.*

Then again Viking warriors in Valhalla drank mead from their enemies’ skulls. The

Haudenosaunee hunters' ferocity may impress the Allfather.

"Is that what happened to the Midgard Serpent?" Thrud asked Boomer.

"A serpent from the far North was adopted into the Monster Serpent Clan and married their new Clan Mother. He is their war chief. They call him 'The Great Horned Serpent.' His sons are fierce."

"Sons! You mean Jormunganđer is breeding?" Thor gasped.

"He and his wife are young, healthy, and fertile. They brood large clutches of eggs." Boomer said. "We need more hunters to keep their numbers in check. That's why my people sent me here."

Thrud laughed at this. "That sounds like a true Wild Hunt."

"Wild Hunt?"

"We hunt someone who's offended the gods once a year." She shrugged.

"The Thunder Beings only hunt the serpents." Boomer said.

"I guess the Wild Hunt is too wild for you," Thrud shrugged.

"The serpents are enough of a challenge, but it's not as if we're ignorant of anger." Boomer shrugged. "We content ourselves with poor harvests and droughts if the Onkwehon:we displease us.

We might strike a human being with a lightning bolt arrow if they anger us, but most aren't so foolish."

He took lumps of brown crystal and offered them for dessert. Thrud bit into it and her eyes lit up. "It's as sweet as honey, but has an aftertaste I never tasted before."

Thor glanced at the lump.

"The aftertaste gives it an exotic but pleasing favor, Father, even if I've never kenned its like before."

Thor bit into it, and it melted in his mouth with a pleasing and distinctive sweetness. "I wouldn't mind eating this again."

"There'll be more maple syrup candies on Turtle Island," Boomer said.

***

"I'll be going to Turtle Island next spring for their hunt." Thor said at the next convened Thing after he saw Boomer off.

"That's longer than we can spare you." Frigga said.

"The Midgard Serpent has found a wife and is breeding an army of serpents on Turtle Island."

They gave horrified gasps and mutterings.

"Jormunganderr has bairns?" Loki asked. Thor had hoped the Trickster would avoid the Thing as he ignored all others. Though he was there because he wanted to hear Thor's report.

Odin's brows furrowed.

"The Haudenosaunee Thunder Beings cull the Monster Serpents in their land each year. They've become more numerous than usual. That's why they invited me to their next Spring Hunt."

"Will they expect you to take part in all their spring hunts?" Odin asked.

"I've only been invited to one spring hunt. I'll decline others if they invite me, but it's best to nip the Midgard Serpent's plans in the bud."

Loki rubbed his hands together. “It’ll be a chance to bring the Wild Hunt to Vinland. I look forward to expanding our hunting grounds.”

Odin nodded, “Very well, Thor, you can be our advance scout for new hunting grounds for the Wild Hunt.”

About the Author

Cathy Smith is a Mohawk writer who lives on a Status Reservation on the Canadian Side of the Border.

You can follow her at:

Wordpress: bit.ly/2e41qWT

Facebook: bit.ly/2dP3rXd

Twitter: @khiatons

Instagram:@cathy2891

Tumblr: bit.ly/2G3dEjo

Pinterest: https://www.pinterest.com/Khiatons/

Tiktok: bit.ly/3KoGwBf

Sign up to the Cathy Smith-Khiatons-I Write Substack https://bit.ly/4qATMGH to receive news and excerpts of new publications and promotions.

www.ingramcontent.com/pod-product-compliance
Lightning Source LLC
Chambersburg PA
CBHW031934260726
48782CB00064B/183

9798230499824